Horton and the KWUGGERBUG
and More Lost Stories

HORTON and the KWUGGERBUG

and More Lost Stories

by Dr. Seuss

Introduction by CHARLES D. COHEN

RANDOM HOUSE 🏠 NEW YORK

Published in the United States by Random House Children's Books,
a division of Random House LLC, a Penguin Random House Company, New York.

The stories and illustrations in this collection were originally published
separately in a slightly different form in *Redbook* magazine:
"Horton and the Kwuggerbug" in January 1951,
"Marco Comes Late" in September 1950,
"How Officer Pat Saved the Whole Town" in October 1950,
and "The Hoobub and the Grinch" in May 1955.

Visit us on the Web!
Seussville.com
randomhousekids.com

Educators and librarians, for a variety of teaching tools, visit us at
RHTeachersLibrarians.com

Library of Congress Cataloging-in-Publication Data
Seuss, Dr.
[Short stories. Selections.]
Horton and the Kwuggerbug and more lost stories / by Dr. Seuss ;
introduction by Charles D. Cohen. — First edition.
 pages cm.
Summary: "A collection of 'lost' stories written and illustrated by Dr. Seuss and
published in magazines in the 1950s. Includes an introduction by Seuss scholar
Charles D. Cohen." —Provided by publisher.
ISBN 978-0-385-38298-4 (trade) — ISBN 978-0-375-97342-0 (lib. bdg.)
1. Children's stories, American. [1. Stories in rhyme. 2. Short stories.] I. Title.
PZ8.3.S477Hoq 2014 [E]—dc23 2014003038

Printed in the United States of America
10 9 8 7 6 5 4 3 2 1   First Edition

Contents

Introduction

CHARLES D. COHEN *graduated from Haverford College and the Tufts University School of Dental Medicine. He's spent twenty-five years practicing dentistry and 25,000 hours studying the life and work of Ted Geisel. Dr. Cohen is the author of* The Seuss, the Whole Seuss, and Nothing but the Seuss, *the definitive work on Ted Geisel, which* Time *magazine named the Best Pop Culture Book of 2004. He has compiled the most comprehensive private collection of Seussiana in the world, and he shares it through loans to galleries and museums and through contributions to books like* The Bippolo Seed and Other Lost Stories *by Dr. Seuss.*

One of my most vibrant childhood memories is the sensation I'd have when opening a Dr. Seuss book for the first time. Each new story brought electric anticipation of the wonders I'd encounter. When Ted Geisel died in 1991, I assumed that I would never experience that thrill again.

Happily, I was mistaken. As it turns out, Ted Geisel published a series of short works in magazines during the 1950s. For the most part, those magazines were tossed out when the next month's issue arrived, and the stories were largely forgotten.

After tracking down and purchasing copies of the magazines, I experienced that old expectant delight, holding what were, to me, "new" Dr. Seuss stories! In 2011, Random House published seven of these gems in *The Bippolo Seed and Other Lost Stories.* It was the first book of tales completely written and illustrated by Ted Geisel to be published in the twenty years since his death, and it became a *New York Times* bestseller.

But as much fun as it is to read a new Dr. Seuss story, there's an equal thrill in revisiting beloved Seuss characters and settings. And in this collection, you get both: stories you're unlikely to have read, each featuring a familiar element. If you loved Marco's marvelous trip down Mulberry Street or his imaginative musings by McElligot's Pool, you'll likewise love learning why he's late for school in "Marco Comes Late." Mulberry Street is also the setting for "How Officer Pat Saved the Whole Town," in which a keen-eyed police officer just may rescue his town from obliteration. Horton fans who rooted for him when he hatched the egg and heard a *Who* can now cheer for him when he confronts a crafty insect in "Horton and the Kwuggerbug." And in "The Hoobub and the Grinch," you'll meet a different Grinch from the one who stole Christmas—but one who similarly believes that everyone is a mindless consumer who can be manipulated.

These tales come from a batch of stories published in *Redbook*. Some of Ted's *Redbook* stories, such as "The Sneetches," "Yertle the Turtle," "Gertrude McFuzz," "The Zax," "The Big Brag," and "If I Ran the Zoo," are well known because he used them later in his books. Others were never published in Seuss books, although that was not due to a lack of interest on the part of Ted or his publisher, Random House.

On September 14, 1956, a month before the publication of *If I Ran the Circus,* Ted signed a contract with Random House for a book called *How Officer Pat Saved the Town and Other Stories.* Although the book was intended for publication in the fall of 1957, few people have ever heard of Officer Pat, and no one has ever seen that book.

At the time he signed the *Officer Pat* contract, Ted had another book scheduled to come out six months later, in early 1957. He had written a letter expressing his excitement about that book: "Don't ever show this letter to anyone, but I've got a hunch . . . (very immodest) . . . we've got a possibility of making a tremendous noise in the noisy discussion of Why Johnny Can't Read . . . [but] the big noise may never come off."

Well, the big noise *did* come off. The new book was *The Cat in the Hat,* and it changed the way generations of children would learn to read. A few months after the book was published, the *Saturday Evening Post* ran a multipage feature story on Ted, and three months later, Random House published *How the Grinch Stole Christmas!* Suddenly, Ted had so much fan mail that it had to be measured in pounds instead of envelopes! It may be hard to imagine, since emails and tweets don't weigh anything, but in 1957 alone, Random House received 9,267 pounds of Dr. Seuss fan mail!

Since that's more than twice the weight of an average-sized car, you can see how dramatically Ted's career changed in 1957. On December 18, two months after *Grinch* was published, Ted signed a contract replacing the *Officer Pat* book with *Yertle the Turtle and Other Stories.*

As a result, stories like "Officer Pat" have essentially been missing for more than half a century. But in this book, not only do we get to enjoy these lost stories, but we also get to see the kinds of changes Ted intended as he developed some of them after publication in *Redbook*. The "Officer Pat" illustrations used in this edition, which come from the archives of the Dr. Seuss Collection at the University of California at San Diego, show some variations from those in *Redbook* and are believed to have been intended for the *Officer Pat* book, before that contract was dissolved in favor of *Yertle.*

Marco, Ted's first children's book character, debuted in September 1937 in *And to Think That I Saw It on Mulberry Street.* The character had such a vivid imagination that when the book was adapted as a half-hour radio broadcast in December 1940, Marco and his imagination were separate roles, voiced by two different actors.

Similarly inspired, Deems Taylor wrote the classical music score *Marco Takes a Walk (Variations for Orchestra)*, op. 25, which premiered in November 1942 at Carnegie Hall and later played in cities around the United States, Canada, and England. Marco's movie debut came in summer 1944 with George Pal's adaptation of *Mulberry Street* as a cartoon short, which was nominated for an Academy Award.

In September 1947, Marco fantasized about fanciful fish in *McElligot's Pool*—the first Dr. Seuss book to contain illustrations with a full-color palette, rather than flat blocks of color, and the first to be awarded a Caldecott Honor.

After these varied adventures, Marco returned in "Marco Comes Late" (September 1950), Ted's fourth story for *Redbook*. Marco's inventive personality stands in stark contrast to the lovable but pedestrian Charlie Brown, who debuted in Charles Schulz's *Peanuts* comic strip one month later. While Charlie Brown suffers through the *wah-wah-wah* voices of authority figures, Marco uses his originality to create escapist dreamworlds. In that way, he's more like Snoopy. When Marco's teacher confronts him for being more than two hours late for school, Marco explains that he left home intending to "be the first pupil to be in my seat. Then *Bang!* Something happened on Mulberry Street!" What follows is a charming account of a journey from Marco's home to school, the opposite of the route traveled in his first book. Marco's story is as imaginative as ever, but as in all the best Seuss stories, there is a lesson to be learned, and both Dr. Seuss and Marco's teacher make sure to differentiate between creative stories and outright lies.

Marco wasn't the only Seussian character whose route took him along Mulberry Street. One month after "Marco Comes Late"—while Random House was publishing *If I Ran the Zoo*—"How Officer Pat

Saved the Whole Town" appeared in the October 1950 *Redbook*. In this story, we meet many denizens of Mulberry Street, including Mrs. McGown and her triplets, Tom, Tim, and Ted; Mrs. Minella with her umbrella; and the vigilant policeman, Officer Pat, who manages to keep disaster from befalling them.

The trouble begins with a fly. Although the structure of "How Officer Pat Saved the Whole Town"—and its insect instigator—may remind readers of "There Was an Old Lady Who Swallowed a Fly," this story preceded that children's song by two years. Of course, Ted didn't invent the subgenre in which sequentially larger things pose ever-increasing dangers. But he was appropriately fond of his version.

In the March 31, 1986, issue of *People Weekly,* Ted's artwork was described as "full of Rube Goldberg gadgets, bulgy-eyed whatnots and baffled people." In my dental office, I have a model of a Goldbergian contraption designed to remove a patient's dentures through an elaborate ten-step process involving, among other things, a tennis racket, a vase, and a monkey. Well aware of Goldberg, at age sixteen Ted wrote a surreal piece for his high school yearbook that depicted his friend having a portrait done by Goldberg, with a piano whirling in midair. Thirty years later, "Officer Pat" was a much more finely honed example of the convoluted logic of a Rube Goldberg gadget.

The chain of unexpected events that occur with Goldberg's impractical devices were an influence, but Ted developed his own reputation for strange things that still made sense. By 1940, the dust jacket for *Horton Hatches the Egg,* his fourth children's book, noted that teachers and librarians had given Ted the title "American Master of Logical Nonsense." Ted termed his method "logical preposterosity" when interviewed for the May 11, 1958, *New York Times Book Review.* In an August 11, 1967, interview for *Time,* Ted simplified that mouthful to "logical insanity," which is the description that stuck. The idea was to pursue a ludicrous situation with relentless logic. As Ted explained in the April 6, 1959, issue of *Life:* "If I start with a two-headed animal I must never waver from that concept. There must be two hats in the closet, two toothbrushes in the bathroom and two sets of spectacles on the night table. Then my readers will accept the poor fellow without hesitation and so will I."

More than six decades after Ted signed the contract that would have brought this story into the canon of Dr. Seuss books, we finally get to watch Officer Pat follow that dogged logic and lead us on a Mulberry Street adventure that is as engrossing as Marco's.

Reading "Horton and the Kwuggerbug" here for the first time may make you think of it as the third Horton story. However, it was actually the second story that Ted wrote about Horton. Readers first met the lovable elephant in 1940, when he was guarding Mayzie's egg in *Horton Hatches the Egg.* His encounter with the Kwuggerbug appeared in the January 1951 *Redbook.* It wasn't until 1954 that Horton would hear Jo-Jo's "Yopp" and save *Who*-ville in *Horton Hears a Who!*

When you see the word *Beezlenut,* you may think of *Horton Hears a Who!* and the kangaroo's threat to have the Wickersham Brothers boil the *Whos'* dust-speck world "in a hot steaming kettle of Beezle-Nut oil!" What you may not remember is that a year earlier, in *Scrambled Eggs Super!,* Ted explained that Beezlenut Blossoms are prized for their sweetness.

But Ted first fashioned a story around the sweetness of Beezlenuts and Horton's fondness for them two years before that, in "Horton and the Kwuggerbug." Horton's faithfulness, good nature, and patience are tested when he is suckered into helping a manipulative Kwuggerbug (a situation much like his encounter with the selfish and thoughtless bird in *Horton Hatches the Egg*). Horton is faithful, "one hundred per cent," this time agreeing with the repeated phrase "a deal is a deal." Once Horton has given his word, he won't back out, no matter how unfairly he is treated. So he braves crocodiles and climbs a mountain to keep his promise to the tricky insect. But have no fear—his faithfulness is rewarded once again.

"The Hoobub and the Grinch" appeared in the May 1955 *Redbook.* How Ted came up with the name *Grinch* is open to speculation. After considering the alternative theories, my current belief is that it came from the French word *grincheux,* which means "grouchy" or "like a sourpuss." In 1934, Ted told his alma mater's newspaper, the *Dartmouth,* "I went to the Sorbonne in Paris. But I lasted there just exactly 45 minutes. I discovered that one had to speak French and I couldn't." But it is also true his college writing showed at least a casual knowledge of French and that, during the seventeen months he was in Europe (ostensibly for graduate studies), he spent about four of them on three vacation trips to France. In any case, *grincheux* is certainly the spirit in which Ted later used *Grinch.*

It's always challenging to get anything good from a Grinch. The first one in a Dr. Seuss story is the Beagle-Beaked-Bald-Headed Grinch in *Scrambled Eggs Super!,* a bird that Peter T. Hooper passes by because it isn't laying eggs that day. Two years later, in "The Hoobub and the Grinch," Grinches are creatures who con others into buying things they don't need. This scenario is particularly ironic, because at the time this story was published, Ted was using a gaunt character with an unmistakable sour puss and pointy fingers to sell Holly Sugar! He seems to have been growing aware of the irony, however. He had been designing Holly Sugar billboards for two years before "The Hoobub and the Grinch" was published, but less than a year later, he wrote and illustrated an eight-page pamphlet to support a ban on billboards in his hometown of La Jolla, California! His contract with Holly Sugar was terminated, and Ted ended the advertising career he had begun three decades earlier.

That's right—before his success with children's books, one of

Ted's jobs was in advertising, a career based on convincing people to buy products. It was a profession that he often satirized within his own advertisements. In storyboarding short films for the Ford Motor Company in 1949, Ted referred to "fast slick salesmanship" to sell fictitious cars like the Dibble-Dorber Bubble Top and the Doberman Atom Splitting Roustabout. Ted later subverted this dynamic in *Green Eggs and Ham,* in which the unrelenting pitchman Sam-I-Am turns out to have something worth trying after all. But that is not the case with a Grinch.

The Grinch in "The Hoobub and the Grinch" may not look exactly like his famous Christmas-stealing namesake, but beyond their name, the two are related by their devious intentions and preoccupation with consumerism. They're also related to their creator—the Hoobub's Grinch reflects Ted's feelings about his history in advertising, and Ted explained in a December 1957 *Redbook* interview that he was the model for the Christmas Grinch's attitude. In fact, he provided the magazine with a drawing of himself looking in the bathroom mirror and seeing the Grinch reflected.

In a speech at the U.S. Postal Service's unveiling of the Theodor Seuss Geisel stamp on October 27, 2003, his stepdaughter Lark Dimond-Cates said, "I always thought the Cat [in the Hat] . . . was Ted on his good days, and the Grinch was Ted on his bad days." As with the playful Cat and the grouchy Grinch, Ted's personality encompassed the naive Hoobub and Horton, the crafty and cynical Grinch and Kwuggerbug, and the imaginative Marco and Officer Pat. The four stories you're about to read are similarly paradoxical, being old tales that are probably new to you. These "lost" stories gave me a renewed zest and rekindled the wonder of reading Dr. Seuss. I hope you are similarly inspired by these fresh encounters with old friends and familiar places.

Horton and the Kwuggerbug

It happened last May, on a very nice day
While the Elephant Horton was walking, they say,
Just minding his business . . . just going his way . . .
When a Kwuggerbug dropped from a tree with a plunk
And landed on Horton the Elephant's trunk!

The Kwuggerbug leaned toward the elephant's ear.
"Perhaps you are wondering," he said, "why I'm here.
Well, I've got a secret!" he whispered. "I know
Of a Beezlenut tree where some Beezlenuts grow!"

Beezlenuts! Horton looked up with wide eyes.

Beezlenuts! THIS was a happy surprise!

For, of all of the nuts in that jungle to eat,

The nut of the Beezle, by far, was most sweet!

"But *why,*" Horton asked, "do you tell this to *me*?"

"Well, you see," the bug answered, "my Beezlenut tree

Is rather far off. And I'm not very strong.

I'd get there much quicker if *you* came along.

So I'll make you a deal that I think is quite fair . . .

You furnish the legs and you carry me there;

I'll furnish the brains, show the way to the tree.

Then half of the nuts are for *you*! Half for *me*!"

"A deal!" Horton said with a smile on his face.

"Hold tight and we're off to your Beezlenut place!

Just steer me and show me the best road to take. . . ."

"No road," laughed the Kwuggerbug. "We'll take the lake!"

And he steered the big elephant down to the shore

Of a lake that was thirty miles long. Maybe more.

"Oh-oh!" shivered Horton. "Now wait just a minute.
I can't swim that lake. It has crocodiles in it!
Just look at their terrible teeth. How they flash!
They'll chew me right up into elephant hash!
I think, Mr. Bug, that there surely must be
A *much* safer way to your Beezlenut tree."

"Now, now!" said the Kwuggerbug. "Don't start to squeal.
You promised you'd go. And a deal is a deal."
"Hmmm . . . ," Horton thought. "What he says is quite true.
A deal *is* a deal. I must see the deal through."
So, bravely the elephant dived in that pond
And he swam and he swam for the shore far beyond
While crocodiles snapped and attempted to eat
His tail and his ears and the soles of his feet.
They nipped at his knees! And they nabbed at his chin!
And he thought, as he fought, that he never would win
But he swam and he swum and he held his trunk high
With the Kwuggerbug on it, quite safe and dry.
A terrible fellow! That Kwuggerbug guy
Just sat there and bossed him, "You hustle, now! Hustle!
I furnish the brains and you furnish the muscle!"

So, from ten in the morning till quarter past two
Poor Horton fought on till he finally got through
To the side of the lake where the Beezlenuts grew.
He crawled from the water, tired, battered and wet.
"Now *where*," Horton asked, "are those nuts that I get?"
"Oh," laughed the Kwuggerbug. "You're not there *yet*!

Climb *that*!" said the bug, pointing up in the sky
At a terrible mountain nine thousand feet high!

"Climb *THAT* . . . ?" Horton gulped. "Not the way that *I* feel."
"Tut-tut!" said the bug. "Now a deal is a deal.
And don't start to argue. No *ifs* and no *buts.*
You'll furnish the ride and I'll furnish the nuts."

"The climb," sighed poor Horton, "will kill me, no doubt.
But a deal *IS* a deal, and I cannot back out."
He drew a deep breath and he threw back his shoulders
And dragged his tired legs over rocks and big boulders.
He stumbled and staggered uphill, over stones
That tattered his toenails and bruised all his bones
While the Kwuggerbug perched on his trunk all the time
And kept yelling, "Climb! You dumb elephant, climb!"
He climbed. He grew dizzy. His ankles grew numb.
But he climbed and he climbed and he clum and he clum.
His hearing grew faint. And his eyesight grew dim.
But he clum and he clum and he clim and he clim
From quarter past two until four-forty-five
Till, finally, old Horton, more dead than alive,
Had carried that bug to the very tip-top
And then, only then, did the elephant stop.
And he gasped to the bug, as he sank to his knees,
"Now where are my Beezlenuts, sir, if you please?"

"Right there!" said the bug. Horton looked. It was true.
'Twas the Beezlenut tree where the Beezlenuts grew!
"But, Bug!" Horton moaned. "We're *here* and they're *there*!
Way out on that peak, and between us is air!
Now *how* can I get through that space in between?
I can't walk on air, if you see what I mean!"

"A deal is a deal," snapped the bug. "I'm the boss.
You stretch out your trunk and you *put* me across!
Stretch, Horton! *STRUTCH!*" yelled the bug. So he strutch.
He strutch it two feet, but it *still* wouldn't touch.
"*Streech,* Horton! *STREECH!*" yelled the bug. So he streeched.
It hurt him real badly, but finally it reached.
"At last!" sang the Kwuggerbug, chuckling with glee,
And he slid down the trunk to his Beezlenut tree.

And he picked all those nuts and he stacked a big mound
Of luscious, sweet Beezlenuts high on the ground.
"But, hey!" called the elephant. "You! Over there!
Half of that mound, don't forget, is my share!"
"Not yet!" said the bug. "All the nuts have been stacked
But, before we can share, they have got to be cracked!"
So he cracked all the nuts. Then he said with a laugh,
"A deal is a deal, and I'm giving you half.
One half of each nut, as you know, is the meat.
And *that* is the half I am keeping to eat.
But half of each nut, as you know very well,
Is the half of the nut that is known as the shell.
The shells are for you!" laughed the bug. And he rose
And he stuffed all the shucks up the elephant's nose!

Now, what would YOU do
If he did that to YOU . . . ?
With shucks up your nostrils, how dreadful you'd feel!
But you couldn't complain. 'Cause a deal is a deal.
You'd have to act terribly nice and do right
So you'd say in a voice that was very polite,
"Thanks, Mr. Kwuggerbug! Thank you for these.
But they tickle my nose. *So look out! I shall sneeze!*"
And you'd sneeze and you'd sneeze!
And you'd snizz and you'd snizz!

And blow all the shucks from your trunk with a *WHIZZ*,
Just the way Horton did. 'Cause they blew out of *his*
And they blasted that Kwuggerbug *so* far away
That he sailed thru the air for the whole month of May
And didn't come down till the fifteenth of June,
All tattered and torn in the late afternoon,
At a place that's *SO* far, now he *never* can go
To his Beezlenut tree where his Beezlenuts grow.

Marco Comes Late

"Young man!" said Miss Block.

"It's eleven o'clock!

This school begins promptly at eight-forty-five.

Why, *this* is a terrible time to arrive!

What's wrong with you, boy? Is your head made of wood?

Why didn't you come just as fast as you could?

What *IS* your excuse? It had better be good!"

Marco looked at the clock.

Then he looked at Miss Block.

"Excuse . . . ?" Marco stuttered. "Er . . . well . . . well, you see,

Er . . . Well, it's like this. . . . Something happened to me.

This morning, Miss Block, when I left home for school,
I hurried off early according to rule.
I said when I started at quarter past eight
I *must* not, I *will* not, I *shall* not be late!
I'll be the first pupil to be in my seat.
Then *Bang!* Something happened on Mulberry Street!

I heard a strange 'peep' and I took a quick look
And you know what I saw with the look that I took?
A bird laid an egg on my 'rithmetic book!

I couldn't believe it, Miss Block, but it's true!
I stopped and I didn't quite know what to do.
I didn't dare run and I didn't dare walk.
I didn't dare yell and I didn't dare talk.
I didn't dare sneeze and I didn't dare cough.
Because, if I did, I would knock the egg off.
So I stood there stock-still and it worried me pink.
Then my feet got quite tired and I sat down to think.

And while I was thinking down there on the ground,
I saw something move and I heard a loud sound
Of a worm who was having a fight with his wife.
The most terrible fight that I've heard in my life!
The worm, he was yelling, 'That boy should not wait!
He *must* not, he *dare* not, he *shall* not be late!
That boy ought to smash that egg off of his head.'
Then the wife of the worm shouted back—and *she* said,
'To break that dear egg would be terribly cruel.
An egg's more important than going to school.
That egg is that mother bird's pride and her joy.
If he smashes that egg, he's the world's meanest boy!'

And while the worms argued 'bout what I should do
A couple big cats started arguing, too!
'You listen to me!' I heard one of them say.
'If this boy doesn't go on to school right away
Miss Block will be frightfully, horribly mad.
If the boy gets there late, she will punish the lad!'
Then the other cat snapped, 'I don't care if she does.
This boy must not move!' So I stayed where I was
With the egg on my head, and my heart full of fears
And the shouting of cats and of worms in my ears.

Then, while I lay wondering when all this would stop
The egg on my book burst apart with a *POP!*
And out of the pieces of red and white shell
Jumped a strange brand-new bird and he said with a yell,
'I thank you, young fellow, you've been simply great.
But, now that I'm hatched, you no longer need wait.
I'm sorry I kept you till 'leven o'clock.
It's really my fault. You tell *that* to Miss Block.
I wish you good luck and I bid you good day.'
That's what the bird said. Then he fluttered away.

And *then* I got here just as fast as I could
And that's my excuse and I think it's quite good."

Miss Block didn't speak for a moment or two.
Her eyes looked at Marco and looked him clean through.
Then she smiled. "That's a very good tale, if it's true.
Did *all* of those things *really* happen to you?"

"Er . . . well," answered Marco with sort of a squirm.
"Not *quite* all, I guess. But I *did* see a worm."

How Officer Pat Saved the Whole Town

The job of an Officer of the Police
Is watching for trouble and keeping the peace.
He has to be sharp and he has to be smart
And try to stop trouble before it can start.
And that's why, one morning, while out on his beat
On the corner of Chestnut and Mulberry Street
He got sort of worried, did Officer Pat,
When his very keen eyes spied a very small gnat
Going *BUZZ!* round the head of old Thomas, the cat.
"Aha!" murmured Pat. "I see trouble in *that*!

If that gnat bites that cat, and he might very well,
That cat will wake up and he'll let out a yell.
That's only *small* trouble. I know it. But, brother,
One small bit of trouble will lead to another!

The trouble with trouble is . . . trouble will spread.
The yowl of that cat will wake Tom, Tim and Ted,
Those terrible triplets of Mrs. McGown.
Then *they'll* yowl a yowl that'll wake this whole town.

When trouble gets started, it always starts more!
Those kids with their racket and ruckus and roar
Will frighten the birds, and the birds will come flapping
Down Mulberry Street with a yipping and yapping!

Once trouble gets going, it spreads just like fire!
Those birds will come screaming toward Mr. McGuire,
The fish-market man. And he'll get such a scare
He'll toss that big codfish up high in the air!

That's the trouble with trouble.
  It grows and it grows.
That fish-in-the-air
  will land smack on the nose
Of that horse over there
  that belongs to Bill Hart.
The horse will start kicking
  Hart's wagon apart
And pumpkins will bounce
  on the head of Jake Warner,
Who's fixing that hydrant
  down there on the corner!
And once all those pumpkins
  start falling on Jake,
He'll fall on his wrench
  and the hydrant will break.
There's no stopping trouble,
  once trouble gets going.
When hydrants get broken,
  the water starts flowing!

The water will gush right on Mrs. Minella.
She'll think that it's rain and put up her umbrella!
And *that'll* knock young Bobby Burke off his bike.
He'll fall on the ladder of House-Painter Mike!
And House-Painter Mike, when he tumbles, will spill
A bucket of paint on the head of Don Dill.
Oh, once it gets started, there's no stopping trouble!
That splashing of paint will upset Mrs. Hubble.
She'll drop all her dishes. They'll smash on the ground
And startle her dog, and the poor frightened hound
Will jump in the horn of old Horn-Tooter Fritz . . .

And Fritz will fall backward and scare Driver Schmitz
On his Dynamite Truck almost out of his wits!
And that Dynamite Truck, with its big load of blitz,
Will race toward that tree and, oh boy! when it hits
The whole of this town will be blown to small bits!"

But lucky for us, down on Mulberry Street,
Good Officer Pat was awake on his beat.
And, quick, the brave officer swung his big bat
On the troublesome head of that troublesome gnat
And kept him from biting old Thomas, the cat,
And stopped all the trouble before it began.
He saved the whole town! What a very smart man!

The Hoobub and the Grinch

The Hoobub was lying outdoors in the sun,
The wonderful, wonderful, warm summer sun.
"There's *nothing*," he said, "quite as good as the sun!"
Then up walked a Grinch with a piece of green string.
"How much," asked the Grinch, "will you pay for this thing?

You sure ought to have it. You'll find it great fun.

And it's worth a lot more than that old-fashioned sun."

"Huh . . . ?" asked the Hoobub. "Sounds silly to me.

Worth more than the sun . . . ? Why, that surely can't be."

"But it *is*!" grinned the Grinch. "Let me give you the reasons.

The sun's only good in a couple short seasons.

For you'll have to admit that in winter and fall

The sun is quite weak. It is not strong at all.

But this wonderful piece of green string I have here

Is strong, my good friend, every month of the year!"

"Even so . . . ," said the Hoobub, "I still sort of doubt . . ."

"But you *know*," yapped the Grinch, and he started to shout,

"That *sometimes* the sun doesn't even come out!

But this marvelous piece of green string, I declare,

Can come out of your pocket, if you keep it there,

Anytime, day or night! Anyplace! Anywhere!"

"Hmm . . . ," said the Hoobub. "That *would* be quite handy. . . ."

"This piece of green string," yelled the Grinch, "is a dandy!

That sun, let me tell you, is dangerous stuff!

It can freckle your face. It can make your skin rough.

When the sun gets too hot, it can broil you like fat!

But this piece of green string, sir, will NEVER do that!

THIS PIECE OF GREEN STRING IS COLOSSAL! IMMENSE!

AND, TO YOU . . .

   WELL, I'LL SELL IT FOR NINETY-EIGHT CENTS!"

And the Hoobub . . . *he bought!*

(And I'm sorry to say

That Grinches sell Hoobubs such things every day.)